1812
Caroline
TAKES A CHANCE

BY KATHLEEN ERNST
ILLUSTRATIONS ROBERT PAPP
VIGNETTES LISA PAPP

★ American Girl®

THE AMERICAN GIRLS

1764  KAYA, an adventurous Nez Perce girl whose deep love for horses and respect for nature nourish her spirit

1774  FELICITY, a spunky, spritely colonial girl, full of energy and independence

1812 CAROLINE, a daring, self-reliant girl who learns to steer a steady course amid the challenges of war

1824  JOSEFINA, a Hispanic girl whose heart and hopes are as big as the New Mexico sky

1853  CÉCILE AND MARIE-GRACE, two girls whose friendship helps them—and New Orleans—survive terrible times

1854  KIRSTEN, a pioneer girl of strength and spirit who settles on the frontier

1864  ADDY, a courageous girl determined to be free in the midst of the Civil War

1904  SAMANTHA, a bright Victorian beauty, an orphan raised by her wealthy grandmother

1914  REBECCA, a lively girl with dramatic flair growing up in New York City

1934  KIT, a clever, resourceful girl facing the Great Depression with spirit and determination

1944  MOLLY, who schemes and dreams on the home front during World War Two

1974  JULIE, a fun-loving girl from San Francisco who faces big changes—and creates a few of her own

Published by American Girl Publishing
Copyright © 2012 by American Girl

Questions or comments? Call 1-800-845-0005, visit **americangirl.com**,
or write to Customer Service, American Girl, 8400 Fairway Place,
Middleton, WI 53562-0497.

Printed in China
12 13 14 15 16 17 LEO 10 9 8 7 6 5 4 3 2 1

All American Girl marks, Caroline™, and Caroline Abbott™
are trademarks of American Girl.

Deep appreciation to Constance Barone, Director, Sackets Harbor Battlefield
State Historic Site; Dianne Graves, historian; James Spurr, historian and First Officer,
Friends Good Will, Michigan Maritime Museum; and Stephen Wallace, former Interpretive
Programs Assistant, Sackets Harbor Battlefield State Historic Site.

PICTURE CREDITS
The following individuals and organizations have generously given permission to
reprint images contained in "Looking Back": p. 77—courtesy of the Toronto Public Library,
Osborne Collection of Early Children's Books; pp. 78–79—© The Metropolitan Museum of Art/
Art Resource, NY (stagecoach on New Jersey road); North Wind Picture Archive (settlers);
photo of artwork courtesy of National Park Service, Nez Perce National Historical Park,
NEPE-1773 (Lewis and Clark meeting Nez Perce Indians); courtesy of the Library of Congress,
LC-USZ62-1236 (coach at inn); pp. 80–81—*Ships in Ice Off Ten Pound Island, Gloucester* by Fitz
Hugh Lane, © Burstein Collection/Corbis; North Wind Picture Archive (post rider); pp. 82–83—
© Darrell Gulin/Corbis (mountain lion); © Susan Rosenthal/Corbis (inlet of Moss Lake);
courtesy, The Winterthur Library: Printed Book and Periodical Collection, detail (woman
caring for the sick); © Leonard de Selva/Corbis (ceramic pharmacy pot).

Cataloging-in-Publication Data available from the Library of Congress

FOR SCOTT AND MEGHAN,
FOR THEIR FAITH AND SUPPORT

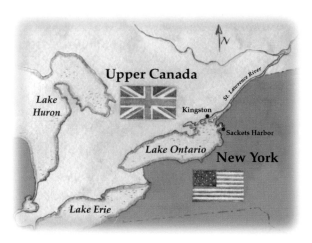

Caroline Abbott is growing up in Sackets Harbor, New York, right on the shore of Lake Ontario. Just across the lake is the British colony of *Upper Canada*.

In 1812, the nation of Canada didn't exist yet. Instead, the lands north of the Great Lakes were still a collection of British colonies. Today, Upper Canada is the Canadian province of Ontario.

In Caroline's time, there was a colony called *Lower Canada*, too. It stretched from Upper Canada eastward to the Atlantic Ocean. Today, it's the province of Quebec.

TABLE OF CONTENTS

CAROLINE'S FAMILY AND FRIENDS

CAROLINE'S FAMILY

PAPA
Caroline's father, a fine shipbuilder who has been captured by the British

MAMA
Caroline's mother, a firm but understanding woman

CAROLINE
A daring girl who wants to be captain of her own ship one day

GRANDMOTHER
Mama's widowed mother, who makes her home with the Abbott family

RHONDA
A twelve-year-old girl who boards at the Abbotts' house

HOSEA BARTON
*A skilled sailmaker at
Abbott's Shipyard*

MR. TATE
*The chief carpenter at
Abbott's and a good friend
of Caroline's family*

SETH
*A young post walker who
delivers mail to nearby
farms and villages*

IRISH JACK
*The captain of a boat
that carries supplies
to Sackets Harbor*

CHAPTER
ONE

—

A SPRING
ADVENTURE

Caroline Abbott smiled as she walked
down the hill in the little village of
Sackets Harbor, New York. *Finally,* a
soft spring day had arrived! The winter had been
long and icy, and then hard rains had pelted the
countryside. Today, though, May sunshine sparkled
on the blue-green waters of Lake Ontario.

Soon the "Abbott's" sign that hung above her
family's shipyard came into view. Caroline's mother
had been in charge of the shipyard for almost a year
now—ever since war had broken out and Papa had
been captured by the British. Caroline missed Papa
terribly. She was also very proud of Mama, who had
kept the business going.

1

Caroline shielded her eyes with her hand and squinted over the water. Almost all travel to and from Sackets Harbor involved ships on Lake Ontario. Now that the winter's ice had melted, the first supply boats of the year would arrive any day. That would be something to celebrate!

Caroline was concentrating so hard that she didn't see Hosea Barton, the sailmaker, until he walked from the yard. "Good morning, miss," he said. "See any boats out there?"

"Not yet," Caroline sighed. "I was hoping to see Irish Jack's boat. He promised Mama last fall that he'd bring supplies for the shipyard as soon as the ice melted. And *I* am waiting to see what new colors of embroidery silk he brings!" Irish Jack was a family friend, and he never failed to tuck a few sewing supplies for Caroline in with his other cargo.

"I hope he comes soon," Hosea said. He sounded more worried than excited.

Caroline looked at her friend. "Is something wrong?"

"We're completely out of sailcloth," Hosea told her. "I have nothing left to work with."

Caroline stared at him with dismay. She hadn't

"See any boats out there?" asked Hosea, the sailmaker.
"Not yet," Caroline sighed. "I was hoping to see Irish Jack's boat."

realized how badly the supply boats were needed. "Did Mr. Tate send you home?" she asked anxiously.

"No, child," Hosea assured her. "I'm running an errand for him. Mr. Tate is trying to keep me busy. We're all waiting to see Irish Jack's boat, though. We're desperate for the supplies he's carrying." Hosea tipped his hat and continued on his way.

Caroline walked slowly into the shipyard. Since war had been declared, the workers had been busy making gunboats for the American navy. It was usually a treat to spend time here—Caroline liked watching the men turn pieces of wood and bits of iron into huge ships. Now, though, the spring afternoon no longer seemed quite as sweet.

In the shipyard, Caroline saw Mr. Tate talking to Mama. "I'm sorry, Mrs. Abbott," he was saying, "but if those supplies don't come in the next few days, we'll have to close the yard. We need bolts, nails, tar, paint... without them, we can't work."

"Let's pray our supply boat arrives, then," Mama told him. "We have to finish that gunboat."

Mama went into the office and closed the door behind her. As Caroline watched Mr. Tate walk away, she thought about what she'd heard. Her chest suddenly felt fluttery inside as a new worry struck her. *The supply boat being late is bad enough,* she thought. *But what if Irish Jack doesn't arrive at all?* Caroline knew that British ships were always prowling Lake Ontario, looking for American boats to capture or sink. Now she realized that Irish Jack's boat would be a special prize. An enemy captain could take Jack and his men prisoner—and deliver all those supplies to the British across the lake in Upper Canada!

Caroline tiptoed closer to the office and peeked in the window. Mama sat on the stool in front of Papa's desk, her face in her hands. Caroline knocked on the door, then opened it. "Mama?" she called. "It's me."

Mama sat up straight, looking startled. "Oh! Caroline, I—I didn't know you were coming today." She picked up a stack of papers and tapped the edges on the desk to straighten them.

"Grandmother said I might," Caroline explained.

Mama nodded. But she looked as if her mind was somewhere else.

"I heard you talking with Mr. Tate," Caroline said. "And Hosea told me that he's used the last of the sailcloth. Could you borrow some supplies from the navy shipyard?"

"I asked." Mama shook her head. "The navy shipbuilders have nothing to spare for us. *Everyone* is waiting for the supply boats. The soldiers and sailors are even running low on food! The supply boats will bring them barrels of salt pork and bags of pilot bread." She sighed. "At least we have our garden. Still, if Irish Jack doesn't come soon, our shipyard will be in trouble."

Caroline swallowed hard as she imagined Irish Jack's dangerous trip to Sackets Harbor. "Do you think the British might have captured his boat?"

"It's possible," Mama admitted. "But perhaps he's just been delayed by bad weather. All we can do is wait."

Caroline nodded, but Mama's answer didn't make her feel any better. Since the war began, she sometimes felt as if she spent all her time waiting. Waiting for news. Waiting for the supply ships. And most of all, waiting for Papa to come home. Waiting could be so *hard*.

"Let's get to work," Mama said. "I've written a letter, but before I post it I'd like you to make a copy for our records. It will be good penmanship practice for you."

Caroline worked with Mama for the rest of the afternoon. After copying the letter, she dusted Papa's books. Keeping busy didn't chase the worries from her mind, though.

As Caroline left the office, she took a hard look around the shipyard. The war had brought Abbott's more business than ever. Caroline watched several carpenters checking measurements on the gunboat they were building. She smelled pine pitch and tar, fresh paint and varnish. The yard rang with saws whining, mallets pounding, men whistling. Caroline couldn't bear the thought of Abbott's Shipyard going still and silent. The American navy needed that gunboat to fight the British!

Caroline trudged home with her head bent. As she approached her house, she saw her good friend Rhonda Hathaway standing by the gate. Rhonda, her little sister Amelia, and Mrs. Hathaway had been lodging in Caroline's house for months.

"Did you hear anything about the American fighters?" Rhonda called. Almost two thousand sailors and soldiers had recently sailed from Sackets Harbor, hoping to capture forts on the Canadian side of the lake. Rhonda's father, a United States Army officer, had left with them.

"There's no news," Caroline told her friend sympathetically.

"I came outside hoping I might see my father walking down the lane," Rhonda said. "I know it's silly of me to watch for him, but—"

"It's *not* silly," Caroline assured her. "I know exactly how you feel."

Rhonda grabbed Caroline's hand. "Your papa has been gone such a long time! I don't know how you bear it."

Caroline felt the Papa-place in her heart squeeze tight. She gazed in the direction of the British stronghold of Kingston in Upper Canada. The last time she'd seen Papa, he was a prisoner there. When news came last fall that American prisoners might soon be sent far away, Caroline and Mama had made a dangerous trip across Lake Ontario to see him. It was the last time Caroline had seen her father.

Now, seven months later, the ache in her heart had not lessened. Was Papa still alive? Was he huddled in some cold prison? Had he managed to escape? There was no way of knowing.

"I miss him every day," Caroline said finally. "Let's go inside now, all right?"

"You go," Rhonda said. "I'm going to stay out here just a little longer."

After supper that evening, Caroline sat in the parlor with Mama, Grandmother, and the Hathaways. Each of them had some needlework project—even little Amelia, who was stitching her first sampler. Caroline was mending a torn seam in her work apron.

Usually their evenings were filled with conversation, but tonight everyone was quiet. Rhonda sighed loudly and dropped the lace that she was making into her lap. Mrs. Hathaway gave Rhonda a worried look. Then Caroline noticed that Mama's hands had stilled on her knitting, too. Mama was staring into the fire, lost in thought. Only Grandmother, who was hemming a new petticoat, seemed focused and steady.

Caroline hated all the sadness and worry. Grandmother always said to look for ways to help a situation instead of brooding about things that couldn't be changed. *I can't do anything about Irish Jack's supply boat,* Caroline thought, *but I can try to cheer up Rhonda.*

She sat for a moment, considering ideas. Then she smiled. "I would like to go fishing one day soon," she said, breaking the silence. "I can take the skiff."

Everyone looked startled. Mama said, "I don't have time to leave the shipyard, Caroline. And you can't go by yourself."

"No, but Seth should pay us a visit any day now," Caroline reminded her. "He's a good sailor, and he told me last time he was here that he'd been dreaming all winter about getting out on the water with a fishing pole." Her friend Seth Whittleslee was the local post walker, tramping many miles to deliver mail and newspapers to isolated farms and settlements. He was a few years older than Caroline, and a good companion on adventures.

Mama nodded. "Very well, then. If Seth can spare the time, you may go."

Caroline looked at Rhonda. "Will you come with us?"

"Me?" Rhonda blinked. "I don't know how to catch fish."

"Then it's time to learn!" Caroline told her. "Please?" She turned to Mrs. Hathaway. "With your permission."

Mrs. Hathaway looked at Mama. "Are you sure the girls will be safe?"

Mama nodded. "Seth and Caroline know how to handle the skiff."

"Then I think you should go, Rhonda," declared Mrs. Hathaway. "An outing will do you good."

Rhonda still looked uncertain, but she nodded. "All right."

"You'll have fun," Caroline promised.

As everyone settled back to their needlework, Grandmother gave Caroline an approving nod. Caroline smiled, pleased by the silent praise. She had suggested the fishing trip in hopes of helping Rhonda forget her worries for a little while. Now she discovered that *she* felt better, too!

Two days later, Caroline and Rhonda walked to Abbott's Shipyard. They'd made arrangements to meet Seth at the yard for their fishing trip. No supply boat had arrived yet, and Caroline could tell that work on the gunboat was slowing to a halt. The spring weather was still beautiful, though, and she was determined to enjoy it. She could hardly wait to get out on the water!

"Today," Caroline announced, "is going to be a good day." She grabbed Rhonda's hand and swung it back and forth.

Rhonda's eyes sparkled with excitement, but she tightened her grip on Caroline's hand. "I'm a little nervous about going out in such a small boat," Rhonda admitted.

"Don't worry. Papa built the skiff," Caroline told her proudly. "*Sparrow* is the finest little skiff on Lake Ontario. And we'll stay close to shore."

Seth strolled up to them, carrying a small ax, fishing poles, and a tin pail holding worms. "Ready?" he asked.

Rhonda frowned. "You cut only two poles!"

Seth gestured to the ax. "I can easily

cut another. I wasn't sure if you actually wanted to fish."

"I intend to fish," Rhonda informed him.

Caroline grinned. "Well, I intend to catch the biggest fish."

"*I* might catch the biggest fish!" Rhonda protested.

"Even if we don't catch anything, it'll be grand to be on the water," Seth said. He glanced at the unfinished gunboat. "The only thing better than taking out the skiff would be serving on a U.S. Navy ship! I hope we defeat the British for good this year."

"I do too," Caroline agreed. Then she pointed to the shed where Papa's skiff had waited out the winter. "Look! The men are bringing out *Sparrow.*"

Caroline, Seth, and Rhonda hurried over. Seeing the skiff made Caroline's spirits rise even higher. The boat had sharply pointed ends and a flat bottom and was just big enough for three people. The trim had recently been repainted in crisp white, with the word *Sparrow* in blue on both sides.

Mr. Tate joined them to watch workers carry the skiff down to the dock. "She's a first-rate little boat," he said. "How your father loved to go fishing, Caroline! Especially when you went with him."

13

Caroline smiled, recalling happy times with Papa. Together they had often sailed *Sparrow* to Papa's favorite fishing spot, a marshy cove called Mallard Bay. He'd built a little lean-to of tree branches for shelter there, and a fire pit. Once, he'd landed a thirty-pound trout!

"I'll take good care of the skiff," Caroline promised.

Mr. Tate squeezed her shoulder. Then he turned to the men easing the skiff into the water beside the dock. "Have a care, now! We can't have Mr. Abbott finding any scrapes on *Sparrow* when he gets home."

Seth climbed down the ladder to the skiff and tucked his gear away. Rhonda went next, clutching her skirt so that she wouldn't trip. Seth settled her in the rear seat. Then Caroline scampered to her own place in the front.

Seth set the oars carefully into their locks and began rowing. Soon they left the sheltered bay. Once they reached the great lake, the chop of the waves grew stronger, but Seth guided the skiff smoothly along the wooded shoreline. Sunlight glistened on the water, and a fresh breeze ruffled Caroline's hair.

"It's a fine day for an adventure," Rhonda said.

Caroline liked Rhonda's spirit. "If the wind stays fair, we'll be able to run up the sail soon," Caroline said. She was eager to raise the sail. She loved to pretend that she was captain of her own ship!

Seth took another pull on the oars. His long legs were better suited for his job as post walker than for sailing the skiff—sitting on the low seat forced his knees almost to his chin!

"I'm glad you could come with us," Caroline told him.

"My pleasure," he said. "What do you think, Caroline? Should we head for Mallard Bay?"

"No!" The word burst out before Caroline could stop herself. She didn't want to take the others to Papa's fish camp without him. "I mean . . . Mallard Bay is too far for Rhonda's first trip."

"There are plenty of good spots closer to home," Seth agreed. He paused for a moment, water dripping from the oars. "I'm dreaming of fresh lake trout, fried up in butter."

"Grandmother's expecting a whole string of trout," Caroline told him. She turned and scanned the lake ahead. "Oh, careful—watch out for that fallen log, Seth."

Seth began to row again. Caroline leaned to one side carefully, using her weight to help Seth navigate around the log, just as Papa had shown her.

I'm grateful for all you taught me, Papa, she thought. She stroked *Sparrow*'s hull, knowing that Papa's hands had shaped each piece of wood.

"Well, where *shall* we go?" Rhonda asked. "I want to catch some fish!"

"How about the mouth of Hickory Creek?" Seth suggested.

Caroline grinned. The place where Hickory Creek flowed into Lake Ontario was one of her favorite fishing spots, and it wasn't too far away. "Perfect!" she said. "Let's head toward Hickory Creek."

CHAPTER
TWO
—

A DESPERATE RACE

 As the skiff traveled farther along the lakeshore, Caroline watched for familiar landmarks. "There!" she announced. "See that marshy area ahead, Rhonda?" She pointed to a swampy cove where tall grasses and cattails pushed from the water. The shoreline was wooded, with no houses in sight. "That's where Hickory Creek flows into the lake."

Seth began expertly rowing through the grasses. Several ducks launched into the air, scolding Caroline and her friends with noisy *quack-quack-quacks* as they flew away.

"Why is this a good fishing spot?" Rhonda asked.

"Two reasons," Caroline told her. "First, fish like the warmer water flowing from the creek."

"And in just a moment, you'll see the second reason we like this spot," Seth promised.

The skiff swished through clumps of cattails. Caroline reached out to touch the leaves as they passed. She liked the way they felt in her fingers, smooth and firm. Then the skiff gently came to a stop. Beneath them, the hull made a soft scraping sound.

Rhonda looked alarmed. "Have we run aground?"

"We're on a sandbar," Caroline explained. "Look into the water. See?" The skiff rested on a long mound of sand and gravel just underwater. "It's an easy place for us to stop and fish."

"The sandbar almost blocks Hickory Creek as it flows into the marsh and on into the lake," Seth added. "There's one deeper channel that cuts through the sandbar." He pointed to an area near the far shore where the water was dark as it poured through the channel.

"Remember when we waded on the sandbar last summer?" Caroline asked Seth. He laughed, and

Caroline told Rhonda how she and Seth had splashed water at each other.

"We both got soaked!" Seth said. "It makes me cold to think about it."

"But don't worry, Rhonda," Caroline added quickly. "We'll stay dry today."

"Will it take long to catch a fish?" Rhonda asked.

"Not if we're lucky!" Caroline said cheerfully. She felt lucky today. The sun was shining, the air felt warm, and she and her friends were on a fishing trip!

Seth handed each of the girls a fishing pole. A string dangled from each pole, with a wire hook on the end. Then he reached for the tin pail that held the worms.

Rhonda's nose wrinkled. "Will I have to put a worm on the hook myself?"

"Only if you want to be allowed to eat whatever you catch," Caroline teased.

"I'll do the worm for you," Seth told Rhonda.

When he had finished, Caroline showed Rhonda how to cast the hook into the water. "And now, wait until you feel a tug on the line," she explained. "That's how you know you have a fish."

"Will it take long to catch a fish?" Rhonda asked.
"Not if we're lucky!" Caroline said cheerfully. She felt lucky today.

"I hope I catch—" Rhonda stopped suddenly. "Oh, look!" She pointed at a long, low boat that had just come into view. An American flag fluttered from the bateau's single mast. The boat was traveling near the shore, heading toward Sackets Harbor. Rhonda's eyes lit up. "Maybe the American soldiers are returning!"

Seth shook his head. "I don't think so. Since it's by itself, it's most likely a supply boat."

Caroline's hopes soared like a gull. She held her breath, squinting at the bateau until she was able to pick out the red banner flying below the national flag. "It's Irish Jack!" she cried.

"Hurrah!" Rhonda cheered.

"Jack and his men will easily make Sackets Harbor with plenty of time to unload yet today," Seth said. "Watch out, Rhonda, I think your line got tangled in those cattails..." His voice trailed away. "Oh no," he whispered. He pointed straight north, past the marsh to Lake Ontario's open water.

Caroline's heart dropped as she followed his gaze. A sloop had just appeared, and she could see a British flag flying from its tallest mast. "It's an enemy ship," she whispered.

Rhonda's eyes were wide. "It's making straight for us!"

"It's not making straight for *us*," Seth said grimly. "It's making straight for the bateau."

Her heart racing, Caroline eyed the sloop. Seth was right. Although the British sloop was zigzagging to make best use of the wind, its captain was clearly heading toward the American supply boat.

Irish Jack must have seen the enemy sloop, too. His bateau was moving quickly now. It had drawn so close to the marsh that Caroline could see Irish Jack's wild red hair. His crewmen were pulling hard at the oars.

Caroline clenched handfuls of skirt fabric in her fists. "Faster!" she urged the crew.

"Are they trying to run for Sackets Harbor?" Rhonda asked. "Why don't they raise their sail?"

"The wind's against them," Caroline told her. She felt hot inside. "All they can do is row."

"Those blasted British!" Seth said angrily. "I wish I could drive them back to Upper Canada myself!"

Caroline felt the same way. "At least the bateau is close enough to shore that the men can jump off and slip away into the woods. They won't be taken prisoner." That thought gave her a scrap of comfort, but she hated to think of the British capturing the bateau and its precious supplies.

Rhonda squinted. "They don't look as if they're planning to abandon the bateau."

"You're right," Caroline agreed. She frowned in confusion. The Americans were still rowing furiously. The bateau moved along at a good pace. What was Irish Jack doing? Now the bateau was turning, hugging the curving shore toward the marsh. Wouldn't Irish Jack make better time to Sackets Harbor if he kept his boat going in a straight line instead of turning into the marsh?

Suddenly, she understood. "He's heading for the creek!"

Seth leaned forward, watching intently. "Of *course*! That's just what I'd do. Irish Jack grew up nearby. He knows every waterway for miles around."

Rhonda pushed her bonnet back in order to see better. "Isn't the bateau too big to travel up the creek?"

"A bateau rides high in the water," Seth explained.

"It will glide right through that deep channel. But if the British try to follow, they'll risk running their sloop aground on the sandbar. I'd guess Irish Jack could make it maybe half a mile or more before the creek gets too narrow and shallow for them to continue. They'll be safe from the sloop's cannons, anyway."

The British ship was well away but still making its determined progress toward them. "*Go!*" Caroline yelled across the water to Irish Jack and his men. "You can make it!" She hugged her arms across her chest, every muscle tight, wishing she could help them row. The bateau was so close now that she could hear the oars splashing. The men were grunting with effort, bending forward and leaning back in rhythm as they strained to outrun the sloop.

As Irish Jack muscled his bateau perfectly among the cattails and on through the narrow channel, Caroline and her friends cheered. The big man gave them a quick wave before his boat slid into Hickory Creek. Soon the bateau moved around a bend and out of sight.

Caroline turned toward the British sloop. "You've lost!" she crowed, although the sailors were too far away to hear. "Turn back!"

24

But the sloop did not turn back. Caroline's sense of triumph turned to alarm.

"I don't believe it." Seth pounded one fist against his knee. "The captain is going to try to follow Jack!"

"I thought you said his sloop would run aground if he tried to sail into the creek," Rhonda said.

Seth narrowed his eyes, considering. "Normally it would. But the creek is running high from the spring rains. Maybe the captain thinks his sloop *could* make it through the channel. And—"

Rhonda finished the sentence. "And if it does, the British will catch the bateau."

Caroline couldn't bear to see the British seize the supplies that were so desperately needed at the shipyard. But what could she and Seth and Rhonda do? Throw their fishing poles at the sloop? Seth could hardly use his little ax to attack a British sloop armed with cannons!

Caroline closed her eyes, trying to concentrate. *All we need is one idea*, she thought. *Just one good idea . . .*

A gull called harshly. Caroline opened her eyes and saw a lone white gull dive nearby. It startled a turtle that had been sunning itself on a fallen log. Caroline stared at the log and caught her breath. Quickly, she began pulling off her shoes and stockings. "Seth!" she cried. "See that fallen log? We might be able to block the channel with it!"

Seth glanced at the log and yanked off his shoes. "It's a grand idea," he said, "although I don't know if it will work."

"We can *try*," Caroline said stubbornly. "Rhonda, lean to the far side."

Rhonda looked puzzled, but she did as Caroline asked. Caroline swung her legs over the skiff's side and slid onto the sandbar. She yelped as icy water clutched her feet, her shins, her knees. The creek water *was* higher than usual. She could feel the current tugging at her as it flowed over the sandbar.

Seth splashed down beside her. He pulled *Sparrow* higher on the sandbar, making sure it was wedged tight and wouldn't float away.

"Just sit still and you'll be fine," he told Rhonda. "Caroline, I'll haul that log over. You grab any branches you can find."

"I want to help, too!" Rhonda pulled off her shoes and stockings. Seth took her hand as she scrambled into the water.

Rhonda gasped. "Ooh—it's freezing!" Her beautiful skirt billowed like a flower before becoming waterlogged. "I'll look for branches," she said.

"Be sure to stay on the sandbar, where the water isn't too deep," Caroline warned her.

The girls headed toward shore, struggling to move through the cold water. Caroline wished she were as tall as Seth and not wearing long skirts. The sand shifted beneath her feet with every step. "Let's grab that one," she said, pointing to a large branch onshore. The girls retrieved the branch and pulled it over the sandbar to the deep channel.

Seth waded to the log where the turtle had been sunning. With a mighty heave, he managed to tug it free. Caroline held her breath as he floated it back through the cattails.

"Is it long enough to block the channel?" Rhonda asked anxiously as Seth joined them on the sandbar.

"We'll see." Seth pointed the log directly across the channel and shoved it into the water.

The fast-flowing water pushed the log as if it were a matchstick. Instead of sinking straight across the channel, like a closed gate, the log was pushed sideways by the current so that it sank at an angle—

like an open gate. Caroline's hopes sank like the log.

"It's a start," Seth said grimly, "but we'll need a lot more than that log to block the channel."

Caroline quickly passed him the big branch that she and Rhonda had found. "Try adding this!"

Seth pointed the branch and threw it into the channel like a spear, just upstream of the log. The water pushed it against the log. For a moment Caroline was afraid the branch would float away, but it settled underwater. Caroline heaved a sigh of relief. Every stick or branch that got caught against the log would help block the sloop.

"I see another one!" Rhonda called. She and Caroline splashed across the sandbar again, grabbed another dead branch, and pulled it back. Seth added a few more, trying to create a logjam of sticks.

"Will it be enough?" Caroline asked urgently.

"I don't know." Seth shook his head as the rushing creek pushed one of the dead branches free. "The water is higher than I've ever seen it."

Caroline looked over her shoulder. Her heart felt as icy as her toes. The British sloop was so close now that she could make out the figures onboard. "Can you use your ax to chop down a small tree?"

Seth shot a glance at the sloop. "We don't have enough time."

"Do you see anything else we can dump in the channel?" Caroline cried. The three of them scanned the shore.

"There's nothing." Seth clenched his fists. "I think we have to give up."

Give up. Those two words made Caroline so angry that she could almost taste something bitter on her tongue. "No!" she said. "We *can't* let the British get the bateau. Mama needs the supplies, and Irish Jack is probably hauling things for the navy yard, too." Feeling desperate, she looked around for something, *anything*, that they could use to block the channel.

Her gaze landed on the skiff. Suddenly she realized that they did *not* have to give up, not quite yet. Tears blurred her vision, but she blinked them away. "I have one more idea," she told her friends. "We can sink *Sparrow*."

"Caroline, no," Seth protested. Rhonda's eyes went wide.

"We must!" Caroline said fiercely. "If we don't block that channel completely, the sloop might still be able to sail through. We can use the ax to chop a hole in the hull." A single layer of planks formed the skiff's sides and bottom. It would be easy for Seth to break through—and then water would flood into the skiff and sink it.

Caroline began wading through the icy water toward the skiff. Seth and Rhonda splashed after her. When they reached it, Seth grabbed their shoes from the bottom of the skiff, stuffed their stockings inside, and hurled them to dry land.

"We need to tow the skiff to the channel," Caroline said.

Seth snatched the bowline. Rhonda and Caroline grabbed the skiff, one on each side, panting as they struggled to pull it to the channel. *Sparrow* was heavier than Caroline had expected, and their progress was slow. The enemy sloop was gaining on them.

"Quick, Seth, get the ax!" Caroline cried.

An angry shout rang across the water. It sounded close. Caroline didn't dare to glance back at the British sloop.

Seth grasped his ax. "Hold her steady! Don't let the current push her away."

The girls struggled to hold the skiff in place over the deep channel, but the current from Hickory Creek was strong. Caroline knew her aching arms couldn't hold the skiff against the rushing water. "Throw me the bowline!" she shouted to Seth.

Caroline caught the rope Seth tossed to her and reached for the end of the log he'd sunk in the channel. It had come to rest just underwater, and she needed to tie the skiff to it. She could barely see what she was doing through the tumbling water. Her numb fingers felt wooden.

"I can't hold on much longer," Rhonda whimpered.

Caroline tried to remember how to tie a strong knot. Thoughts raced through her mind so fast that she couldn't catch a single one. Panic bubbled up inside. Then she heard Papa's voice in her memory: *Sailors practice their knots so often that when they need to make one quickly, their hands remember how.*

Caroline took a deep breath and tried again. She found that her hands did indeed remember how. Soon the skiff was secured against the log. Caroline knew it would hold long enough for Seth to do his job.

Seth raised his ax. *Whack! Whack! Whack!* The blade made a horrid sound as it bit into *Sparrow*'s hull. A ragged hole opened. Water poured through. As the skiff slowly filled with water, it began to sink into the channel.

Caroline held her breath. If the current pushed the skiff free of the channel, the British might still slip through and capture the bateau—and its precious supplies.

But the heavy skiff did not float away. It stood almost on end as it sank into the channel, lodged against the log and branches already in place. The front end of the skiff settled on the sandy bottom. The back, with the word *Sparrow* gleaming in the sunlight, came to rest just above the waterline. The skiff held firm, blocking the channel.

"Will *that* keep the British from sailing through?" Rhonda asked. She was shivering.

"It must!" Caroline said. She had sacrificed her family's skiff. She couldn't bear to think that it might not save the supply boat.

Seth's chest heaved from his efforts as he scrambled up on the sandbar. "That captain would be a fool to try chasing Irish Jack now," he said.

The blade made a horrid sound as it bit into Sparrow's hull.

"Be on your way," Rhonda told the British captain. She shaded her eyes with one hand, peering intently at the sloop.

Caroline imagined the British officers watching through spyglasses as they tried to decide what to do. The next few moments seemed to pass very, *very* slowly.

Finally the sound of shouted commands drifted across the water. The crewmen adjusted the sails. The sloop turned back toward Upper Canada.

"They're giving up!" Rhonda cried. Seth whooped with joy.

Caroline could hardly believe her eyes—but there was the British sloop, sailing away in defeat. "We did it," she said. "We really did it!"

SETH'S DECISION

Caroline, Rhonda, and Seth sat shivering on the shore, putting on their dry stockings and shoes. They had watched the sloop until it sailed out of sight.

"How are we going to get home?" Rhonda asked.

"We'll have to walk," Seth said.

Now that the first flush of excitement was past, Caroline felt tired all the way to her bones. How far were they from Sackets Harbor?

She jumped as some branches rustled nearby. Then Irish Jack appeared through the trees. A huge grin split his face. "You three are the heroes of the day!" he called. "I got my bateau upstream as far as I could. Then I came ashore and walked back to see what the British would do. I saw how you blocked the channel. That was quick thinking!" He grabbed his hat and slapped it against his leg with delight.

Caroline scrambled to her feet. "It's good to see you," she told him. "Mama and Mr. Tate need those supplies you're carrying. We've been waiting and *waiting*."

Irish Jack shook his head. "We've had a slow trip. British captains have been sailing back and forth, ready to pounce on any American boat they can find. I've had to hide my bateau several times before this."

"You're sure the bateau is safe now?" Caroline asked.

Irish Jack ran a hand through his wild red hair, looking pleased. "Sure as the sun will rise tomorrow. My crew is guarding her. When we're certain that blasted British sloop isn't prowling about, we'll slip on to Sackets Harbor."

"But the channel is blocked now!" Rhonda said. "How will you get out?"

"Oh, we can pass through," Irish Jack promised. "Even loaded, we can pull the bateau right over the sandbar."

"That's g-good," said Rhonda. Her teeth were chattering.

"I've got blankets on my boat," Irish Jack said. "Let's go fetch them. Once you've warmed up a bit, I'll escort you home." He turned and walked back in the direction he'd come, upstream where the bateau was hidden. Seth and Rhonda followed.

Caroline started to bring up the rear, but she paused to take one last look at the channel. She could see the back end of the skiff where it had come to rest, with the word *Sparrow* above the flowing water.

Caroline swallowed hard. Papa had built that skiff! It had taken her and Papa on many happy fishing trips. It had safely gotten her and Mama all the way to Kingston and back last fall. Now she would never skim over the water in it again.

I lost my ship, Caroline thought. Papa always said that a captain who lost his ship was disgraced. What would he think of her now? Caroline's heart seemed to freeze in her chest. She felt mixed up inside—proud and ashamed, happy and sad, all at the same time.

"Caroline?" Rhonda called.

"I'm coming," Caroline answered. She took one last look at the precious skiff. Finally, she forced herself to look away.

Caroline plodded after Irish Jack as he walked her, Rhonda, and Seth home. The bateau captain did not accept Grandmother's offer to come inside for warm gingerbread. "I need to get back to my crew," he said. "But I hope you'll give these three heroes extra helpings. They did a fine thing today."

A fine thing, Caroline thought, *and a terrible thing, too.*

Once Rhonda's mother heard the story, she hurried off to fetch Mama. Grandmother found a pair of old trousers and a shirt that belonged to Caroline's cousin Oliver and gave them to Seth. "Get into dry clothes, all three of you," she ordered. "I'll make hot willow-bark tea. It's the best thing to ward off a fever."

Caroline was glad to peel off her wet dress and to pull on thick, warm stockings. Soon everyone

was gathered in the Abbotts' kitchen except Amelia
Hathaway, who was napping upstairs. A big fire
blazed in the hearth, and steam rose from mugs of
tea. Caroline sat at the table with her winter cape
draped over her shoulders. She let Seth and Rhonda
repeat the tale of their adventure.

"Mercy!" Mrs. Hathaway said, shaking her head.
"I will say a prayer of thanks tonight that none of you
was hurt." She pressed her lips into a tight line as if
imagining what might have been.

"It's sad to lose the skiff," Mama declared, "but
look what was saved! That was sharp thinking."

Normally Caroline would glow with such praise
from Mama, but she could still hear the harsh sound
of splintering wood as the ax fell. She could still see
the word *Sparrow* at a crazy angle above the water,
shining in the sun.

Grandmother pulled a pan of gingerbread from
the brick oven. She cut pieces and passed around
plates. The spicy-sweet smell of warm gingerbread
usually made Caroline's mouth water, but now she
didn't have an appetite.

"The woodbox is almost empty," Grandmother
murmured. "I'll just fetch a few more logs."

Caroline jumped to her feet. "I'll help," she said. She wanted a few moments alone with Grandmother, who often helped her sort through tangled feelings. She followed the old woman outside. Grandmother walked slowly, leaning on her cane. She was a small woman, with hands gnarled like tree roots and bones that often ached.

"Grandmother," Caroline began. "When I saw Papa's skiff ruined, left behind in the creek, I..." She stopped. It was hard to describe how she felt.

Grandmother took Caroline's chin in one hand and looked her straight in the eyes. "I know it's hard to lose the skiff, but you did *well* today," she said fiercely. "The British stole *White Gull*. That was one of the loveliest sloops your father ever built, and it's no doubt been renamed and put into the British fleet! Our enemy has stolen other ships as well. But today, thanks to you and your friends, they did not capture Irish Jack's bateau."

*I **am** proud of what we did,* Caroline thought. But the ache beneath her ribs didn't go away.

Caroline gathered an armload of wood, and Grandmother filled her own apron with smaller pieces. Before heading back inside, Caroline paused.

"I'm tired," she said, scuffing a circle in the dirt with her toe. "After we take the wood in, I think I'll rest for a little while."

Upstairs, Caroline's cat, Inkpot, was curled into a ball on her bed. Caroline lay down and scratched him under the chin. "Oh, Inkpot," she whispered. "We saved Irish Jack's bateau and supplies, but we sank Papa's skiff! It's *ruined.*"

Would Papa be disappointed in her when he heard what she'd done? Caroline wanted so much to talk with him. *If only he were here,* she thought. Tears spilled down her cheeks.

Then, for the first time, the fear that she had pushed away for so many months washed over her: *What if I never get the chance to talk to Papa again?* she thought. *What if he never comes home?*

Before Mama went back to the shipyard later that afternoon, she invited Seth to stay for supper. "Thank you, ma'am. I'd like that," he said. "And I'll be glad to help Caroline with chores until then."

Seth and Caroline grabbed empty buckets and

headed outside. When they reached the well, Seth paused. "I'm sorry about the skiff, Caroline," he said. "I know it meant a lot to you."

Caroline nodded. "Papa made it." Her eyes blurred with tears. "Oh, Seth, what if Papa doesn't come back?"

Seth hooked a bucket handle onto a rope and began lowering it into the well. "Your papa's coming back. Don't stop believing that, Caroline. And he'll understand that you had a hard choice to make when we saw that British sloop headed for the supply boat."

Caroline sighed. "Everything happened so fast."

"We had a grand victory this morning," Seth reminded her. "In fact, what happened back at Hickory Creek helped me make up my mind." He hauled up the full bucket, set it on the ground, and looked at Caroline. "I—I'm joining the navy."

Caroline's eyes widened. Seth? Joining the navy? She knew that boys even younger than Seth sometimes joined the navy. The smallest became "powder monkeys," scampering through a ship's cramped spaces to deliver ammunition during battles. Still, she'd never imagined Seth going off to fight. *But perhaps I should have,* she thought, remembering how he'd spoken of wanting to help drive the British back to Upper Canada.

"I've been thinking about it for some time," Seth said. "Seeing that British sloop chasing Irish Jack's bateau this morning—well, it made me angry! I am resolved to do whatever I can to help win this war."

Caroline wanted to say, *No, don't go! You might get hurt. And I'll miss you too much!* But she managed to swallow the words. "I'm proud of you, Seth," she said instead. "You'll do a fine job in the navy."

When Mama got home from the shipyard that evening, carrying a basket of salmon she'd purchased for supper, Caroline and Seth were hoeing weeds in the garden. "Wonderful!" Mama said. "Thank you, Seth."

Seth wiped his forehead, leaving a streak of dirt. "You've always treated me kindly, Mrs. Abbott. Since I've no family of my own, that means a lot."

"You're always welcome here," Mama assured him with a smile.

Caroline looked at Seth with a silent message:
Tell her your news.

He nodded and told Mama about his decision
to join the navy. "I've been walking my post route
for four years," he explained. "Someone younger can
take that job now."

"When are you leaving?" Mama asked.

"I'll send word to my employer, letting him know
he needs to find another post walker for my route,"
Seth said. "And I've a single day's worth of mail yet
to deliver—the route closest to Sackets Harbor. Then
I'll be free to enlist."

"I could deliver your mail tomorrow," Caroline
offered. "I'd be proud to. That way you could enlist
to fight the British one day sooner."

Mama hesitated.

"I won't get lost," Caroline said. "I know the
route almost as well as Seth." She'd walked this part
of his route with him several times, keeping him
company.

"You'd have to get an early start," Seth told her.
"It will be a long day of walking."

"I don't mind," Caroline insisted. "Please, Mama?
I want to help."

Mama considered. "Very well," she said at last. "You're ten now. Old enough to take on that responsibility."

Caroline nodded. First thing in the morning, she'd be ready to go.

INTO THE WOODS

The next morning, long before the Hathaways were awake, Mama, Grandmother, Caroline, and Seth ate breakfast by candlelight. Then Seth went over the instructions for delivering mail. "Be sure to shout hello before you go into the Randalls' clearing. Their dog doesn't like strangers coming too close to the house. And—"

"I *know*," Caroline said. "You've told me these things five times already!"

"I packed a lunch for you, Caroline," Grandmother said. "Smoked fish, cheese, and bread. Seth, I packed the same for you. I hear the food aboard navy ships isn't so tasty."

"Thank you," Seth said. "It will likely be the best meal I'll have for some time."

Mama was bustling around the kitchen. "Caroline? Perhaps you should take a lantern."

"Must I?" Caroline asked. "It will be dawn soon, and I don't want to carry a lantern all day."

"Pack a candle, then," Mama said firmly. She held out a precious candle and several matches. Caroline tucked them into Seth's waxed canvas mailbag.

"Take a knife as well," Grandmother said. "While you're out, please cut some willow bark for me. Since it's so good for fighting fevers, I always want some handy."

Caroline nodded. "I'll gather what I can." She added a knife to the bag and slung the canvas strap over her shoulder.

The sun hadn't quite crept into the sky when the four of them walked outside, and Caroline shivered in the chilly gloom. Mama and Grandmother stopped to say good-bye at the front gate. "You come back when you can," Grandmother told Seth.

Seth smiled. "Yes, ma'am."

Mama grasped Caroline's shoulders. "Come

straight home when you've finished your deliveries," she said sternly. "You've a long walk ahead of you, and you *must* be home before dark."

Caroline nodded. "I will."

"And stay well clear of strangers," Mama added. "These days there are spies about. Smugglers, too, trying to sneak weapons or supplies between New York and Upper Canada. And deserters—soldiers who have run away from their duty. Let them keep their bad business to themselves."

"I *will*," Caroline promised. "I'll be fine, Mama."

Caroline and Seth walked to Main Street together. From here, Seth would head down to the harbor. Caroline tried to give him a smile. "Please take good care of yourself," she said.

He held out a hand. Instead of taking it, Caroline threw her arms around her friend. Despite Grandmother's best efforts to feed Seth well, Caroline could feel every rib through his shirt. He gave her a quick, tight squeeze. Then he walked away.

Caroline took one deep breath before turning in the other direction. She had a job to do. Besides, staying busy and delivering the mail would help keep her from worrying too much about Seth.

Soon she left Sackets Harbor behind. *I'll try to deliver all of the mail before I eat lunch,* she decided. Then she'd turn around and head home.

As the sun rose, Caroline walked east on a narrow road so rutted and muddy that she was relieved to turn onto a hunting trail. In the thick forest, though, very little sunshine sifted through the leaves. Caroline pulled her wool shawl over her head to keep her ears warm.

Her first stop was a farm tucked into a small clearing, far from the nearest neighbor. A woman was planting her garden, and her husband and son were burning brush to make way for a new field. Caroline tried to walk around the blowing smoke as she approached the cabin. "I brought you a letter!" she called. The woman ran to greet her, smiling with pleasure. Caroline smiled back, feeling as if she'd done something good.

Caroline stopped at several more farms as she headed farther away from Sackets Harbor. After delivering her last piece of mail, she sat on a cliff overlooking Lake Ontario to eat lunch.

She recognized where she was, for she'd often seen this particular bit of high ground from the lake. *I'm not too far from Mallard Bay*, she realized. She remembered spring fishing trips with Papa on days like this, when the woods were full of blooming trees and birds sang pretty songs.

Caroline nibbled some cheese, thinking about the fish camp. She and Papa had usually been alone together at Mallard Bay. After losing the skiff, Caroline wanted more than ever to feel close to Papa. How she longed to visit the camp!

A tempting idea slipped into her mind. She was so close ... why not just go?

A bold chipmunk skittered close, looking for stray crumbs. "But Mallard Bay is in the wrong direction," she told herself. Mama expected her to come straight home. And hadn't she promised Papa, when he was taken prisoner, that she'd obey Mama and Grandmother?

But Caroline didn't *want* to go straight home. More than anything, she wanted to go to Papa's fish camp. If she hurried, Mama would never know.

Caroline stuffed the rest of her lunch back into

the sack, dusted her hands on her skirt, and got to her feet. She'd have to be quick. After hitching the bag over her shoulder, she started walking. She headed farther east instead of back toward Sackets Harbor. Caroline felt a little guilty about disobeying Mama, but the thought of visiting the fish camp again made her tingle with excitement.

Yet Mallard Bay seemed to be farther than she'd thought. She and Papa had always traveled there by boat, so she hadn't realized how long it would take to walk. The path wound through woods near the lake's edge, and with every twist and turn, she hoped to see the familiar fish camp appear in front of her. Each time, her hopes were disappointed.

Finally she thought, *Maybe I should turn back.* The sun was no longer directly overhead—the afternoon was passing. If she didn't get back home before dark, Mama would be angry! Besides, there were wild animals in the woods—cougars and wolves and bears. Caroline shivered. She didn't want to stumble into one of those in the dark! But she didn't want to turn back, either—not when she'd already come so far. *Surely* she was almost there.

She was getting thirsty, so when she spotted

a narrow path leading from the main trail to the lake, she took it. The shoreline here was marshy, but the water was clear and cold. Caroline crouched at water's edge and cupped her hands. For a moment she let her hands stay underwater. How she loved Lake Ontario, and how she had loved sailing with Papa!

Suddenly she heard a low mutter of voices. She froze, eyes wide. Some of the cattails and tall reeds thrashed with a rustling sound.

"I'm bailing as fast as I can," a man's voice complained. "I can't keep up. We need to make camp for the night."

"It's not safe for us to make camp until dark," a second man hissed. "And keep your voice down!"

The front tip of a canoe appeared among the plants. For one startled moment, Caroline stared into the face of a stranger, who sat in the bow with his paddle. He looked as surprised as she felt. Then his face clouded with anger.

"You there!" he shouted. As the canoe slid from the cattails, the man in the back of the canoe came into view also. He scowled at her.

Caroline scrambled to her feet and raced into the woods. She didn't wait to hear if the men gave chase. Instead she plunged deeper into the underbrush. Brambles caught at her hands and cheeks. A low vine or root caught her foot. She tripped and fell with a noisy crash.

Ow! she whimpered silently. For a few moments she couldn't move. Had the men heard her fall? She held her breath, listening hard. She didn't hear anything.

Caroline blinked back tears of pain as she sat up. Thorns had scratched her palms. Worse, her left arm had hit a rock when she fell. Her dress was torn, and blood oozed from a bad scrape near her elbow.

Oh no! she thought miserably. The rip in her sleeve would not be easy to mend, and she saw that several drops of blood stained the fabric. Mama and Grandmother would not be happy.

Caroline stumbled to her feet. Peering back through the trees, she was relieved to see no sign of the two men. They must have stayed down in the marsh. She had to be nearly to Mallard Bay by now.

Papa's fish camp would be a good, safe place to clean the scrape on her elbow. Then she would have to hurry home!

She glanced nervously at the sun again. If she ran most of the way, walking only when she needed to catch her breath, she should be able to get home before dark.

But ... where *was* the trail? Caroline looked around. *I'm lost!* she thought. Fear made her skin prickle and her breath come in little gasps.

She forced herself to take a deep breath and think calmly. *The trail follows the shoreline, roughly,* she reminded herself. Yet she was sure that she hadn't crossed the trail when she ran away from the strangers in the canoe. Looking over her shoulder through the trees, she saw the open sky over the lake. Carefully, she walked away from the lake in as straight a line as she could, making her way around trees and shrubs.

Just when she was starting to get frightened again, she climbed over a large rock and spotted the trail. Caroline blew out a long sigh of relief. She'd never been so glad to see that ribbon of tramped earth before!

Once back on the trail, Caroline was on her way. *Hurry-hurry-hurry*, a voice in her mind whispered. Finally she rounded a bend and saw the quiet, marshy waters of Mallard Bay ahead.

She'd reached Papa's fish camp!

AT THE FISH CAMP

Caroline stopped on the path, taking in the familiar view. There was the little fire pit where Papa had fried his trout. The brush lean-to he'd constructed needed some repair, but it still stood nearby. The hollow log where he left fish lines and hooks seemed undisturbed.

Being here brought tears to her eyes. *This is a special place,* Caroline thought. She and Papa had shared many happy hours here. As she walked through the clearing and down the path to the lakeshore, she felt Papa's presence in her heart.

She knelt by the edge of the water and carefully washed the scrape on her arm. Although it still hurt, it had stopped bleeding. When she got home,

Grandmother would apply a paste made of healing herbs. *And I need to get home fast,* Caroline told herself. Golden sunlight slanted through the trees, casting long shadows.

Several scrubby willow trees grew near the water. Remembering Grandmother's request, Caroline quickly used the knife she'd brought to peel away bits of bark. Then she put them into her sack.

When she walked back to the clearing, Caroline paused for one moment more. She could almost hear Papa laughing. She could almost smell the wonderful aroma of fresh-roasted fish. "I'm still waiting for you to come home, Papa," she whispered. "I haven't given up hope."

As she reluctantly turned to leave, a low moaning sound made her freeze. Was an animal hurt nearby? She looked around the clearing but saw nothing.

The sound came once more. It seemed to be coming from the lean-to. Caroline's skin felt prickly again. She bent over slowly and peered into the lean-to. Someone was lying inside, half-covered with dead leaves.

Caroline didn't know what to do. The man had done his best to hide himself, which meant he didn't want anyone to see him. Was he a smuggler or a spy, or someone else up to no good?

She was about to run from the clearing when the man moaned again. Caroline felt troubled. He must be badly hurt, or sick. She tiptoed closer to the lean-to and peeked beneath the low roof.

A skinny man lay on a torn blanket. His eyes were closed, but he moved restlessly. Caroline studied him. His hair was long and uncombed. A beard covered his chin. The clothing she could see among the leaves was dirty and ragged, and his feet were bare. A tin cup rested on its side near his hand.

The man muttered something in his sleep. His forehead looked wet with sweat. Caroline wondered if he had a fever. She knelt beside the lean-to. The very least she could do for him was refill his cup before she left. *I'll stop at the nearest farm and tell the family about this man,* Caroline decided. The adults there would know what to do.

Holding her breath, she reached inside and retrieved the cup. Then she paused, squinting in the gloom. She didn't recognize the man. Still, there was something about him . . .

The man moaned again. "We must set sail," he muttered.

And then Caroline *knew*. Her heart banged against her ribs. "Papa? *Papa!*"

He didn't answer. She crawled to him and put one hand against his forehead as she'd seen Grandmother do. It *was* Papa—and he was burning with fever.

Caroline knew that if she didn't break the fever, Papa might die. She scrambled from the lean-to and raced to the lake. She ripped off a piece of her torn sleeve and wet it. Then she ran back to the lean-to and laid it over Papa's forehead.

What next? If only Grandmother were here! She would know what to do. Trembling with fear, Caroline tried to think calmly and remember what Grandmother had taught her.

Caroline quickly gathered firewood and then used one of the matches Mama had given her to start a fire. She fetched water from the lake and heated it in the tin cup. She crushed some of the willow bark she'd just gathered and added it to the water. Grandmother usually dried the bark before using it, but this would have to do.

When the tea was ready, Caroline crawled back into the lean-to. "You must drink this, Papa," she said gently. She cushioned his head on her lap and oh-so-slowly helped him sip the tea. Sometimes it spilled down Papa's cheek. By the time the cup was empty, though, she was sure that he'd swallowed some of the healing brew.

Caroline heated more water. Thank goodness she hadn't eaten all of her lunch! She crumbled the leftover bread and fish into the cup. Papa was skinny as an oar. Some soup would help. Her own stomach was beginning to growl, but she fed all of the food to Papa, one tiny sip at a time.

When the cup was empty, Papa seemed to settle into a deeper sleep. Caroline watched him breathe, her heart overflowing. Finding Papa felt like a miracle! But she knew he was very sick. *Did I find him just to lose him again?* Caroline wondered.

A while later, Papa moved. Caroline thought he opened his eyes for a moment, although it was hard to tell in the gloom. "Papa?" she whispered. "It's me, Caroline. Are you feeling better?" But he didn't answer.

By that time, full night was falling like a black

"You must drink this, Papa," Caroline said gently. She cushioned his head on her lap and oh-so-slowly helped him sip the tea.

blanket. Caroline lit the candle, dripped some hot wax on a flat stone, and used that to hold the candle upright. She set the stone just inside the lean-to. The tiny light gave her a bit of comfort.

Although the night was cool, Papa was sweating. Was his fever breaking? She patted Papa's forehead dry with the hem of her skirt, but he didn't waken.

She lay down beside him. The night forest was full of rustles and strange noises, and her thoughts tumbled like pebbles in a creek. Mama and Grandmother must be dreadfully worried by now. *I'm sorry to frighten you*, Caroline told them silently, *but I must take care of Papa*.

Caroline opened her eyes to find a milky new dawn lighting the clearing. She sat up quickly and checked Papa. He was no longer restless, and his skin felt cooler beneath her fingers. Relief flooded through her. His fever had broken!

"Caroline?" Papa whispered. "Is that really you?"

Caroline didn't know whether to laugh or to cry. "It's me, Papa."

"Oh, my dear daughter, I feared I'd never see you again!" Papa blinked, as if he didn't believe his eyes. "How on earth did you find me?"

"I was delivering mail for Seth," Caroline explained. "I was supposed to go straight home yesterday, but I was so close to Mallard Bay, I decided to visit. I never imagined I'd find *you!*" A lump rose in her throat. "But—what are you doing here?"

"I escaped from the British, and I've been making my way home," Papa said in a husky voice. "I got this far, but I couldn't go any farther. I was very hungry. I hoped I might find my fishing line and hooks still tucked into the hollow log. But by the time I got here, I was too weak to use them."

"You've been ill," she told him. "You had a terrible fever last night. How long have you been traveling?"

"A long time," he murmured. "I've been moving slowly. You see, I broke my leg—"

Caroline caught her breath. "You broke your leg?"

"Months ago, now." Papa lifted his hand, then let it drop again. "But it didn't heal well."

Caroline grabbed his hand, almost afraid he'd disappear.

"Your mother, is she well?" Papa asked anxiously.

"She's fine," Caroline assured him. "Everyone is fine." At least they would be, once Caroline and Papa got home! "What *happened*, Papa? How did you escape?"

"The British in Kingston sent many of their prisoners east to Halifax last fall," Papa said. "I knew the trip would be my best chance to escape. We'd sailed far down the Saint Lawrence River before I got a good chance to try. One night I noticed that a guard had gotten drunk. I managed to yank the gun from his hands and crack him on the head with it."

Caroline's eyes went wide. It was hard to imagine her peaceful papa doing that! "Did you kill him?"

Papa shook his head. "No, dear child, but I imagine he lost his senses for a time. I dove over the side of the boat, swam to shore, and hid in the woods. Even though the moon was full that night, the guards didn't try to follow me. I suppose they decided that an American with no weapons or money or even a warm jacket, in British territory, with winter coming down hard, wasn't much of a threat."

Caroline shivered. "How ever did you survive? Where did you go? How—"

"I'll tell you everything in time, I promise." Papa squeezed Caroline's hand gently and closed his eyes. "I need to rest now."

Caroline waited until Papa was sleeping peacefully before creeping from the lean-to. Her head and her heart were full of worries. Mama and Grandmother must be terribly frightened by her absence, yet with Papa so weak and sick, how could she get him home?

If only I had a skiff or even a rowboat, she thought. Traveling by boat was far easier than trudging overland.

Caroline glanced back toward the lean-to, wondering what to do. She could leave Papa sleeping and run to get help, but what if a smuggler or other troublemaker stumbled across the fish camp? What if Papa's fever grew worse again after she left?

I must stay here with Papa, she decided. *I must help him get stronger so that we can go home.*

While Papa slept, Caroline searched the woods nearby until she found a sturdy Y-shaped stick that she thought might work as a crutch. She stuffed

Seth's mail sack with leaves and tied it into the notch to cushion Papa's arm when he leaned against it.

Papa's fishing gear was still in the hollow log. Caroline turned over stones until she found a worm to put on the hook. Then she went down to the shore to try her luck. It seemed to take a very long time to attract a fish, and several times she went back to the lean-to to make sure that Papa was sleeping. Finally she felt a tug on the line. A small whitefish was on the hook. She wanted to shout with joy, but it took all of her concentration to pull the line to shore without the fish getting away.

She had helped Papa and Grandmother clean fish many times. While the whitefish roasted on a stick beside the fire, she gathered some tender fiddlehead ferns growing near the campsite. When the fish was cooked, she made a cup of watery whitefish-and-fern soup for Papa.

By the time that was done, Papa was awake again. She found him sitting up inside the lean-to. "Oh, Papa," she said thankfully, "you're looking better."

"I'm feeling better too," Papa said. He accepted

the soup she offered and slowly drank some. "My, that tastes good. I haven't had a warm meal in so long."

How had he ever survived? It hurt Caroline to imagine Papa hungry—and injured, too. "How did you break your leg?" she asked anxiously.

"I was so eager to cross the Saint Lawrence River and reach American soil that I was careless," Papa told her.

"Careless?" Caroline asked. She'd never known Papa to be careless!

"After I escaped, I began making my way west, staying hidden, waiting for the river to freeze," Papa explained. "I set out as soon as the ice looked passable. I should have waited a few more days, though. I was almost to shore when the ice cracked and opened up right in front of me. I made a mighty leap, trying desperately to make it to the beach. I knew I'd freeze to death if I fell into that water."

Caroline's heart raced, as if she were facing the dangerous jump. Suppose he hadn't made it across?

Papa drained the last of the soup before continuing. "I did make the beach, but I landed on a rock and broke my leg. I would have died there if some Oneida men hadn't found me the next morning. One of them set my leg, and they took me to their village. I spent the winter there with the Indians. By the time the snow finally melted a few weeks ago, I knew my leg was as strong as it was going to get. So I thanked my Oneida friends and began walking home."

"Why didn't you send us word?" Caroline exclaimed.

"I didn't know whom I could trust," Papa said simply. "I knew that some of my old friends remained loyal to the British and might turn me in instead of helping me." He smiled at her. "I learned that lesson from the embroidered map you showed me when you visited me at the prison in Kingston."

Caroline felt proud to know that her handiwork had helped him. She had marked dangerous spots on the map she was embroidering of the eastern end of Lake Ontario. And she'd managed to show Papa the map—right under the guard's nose!

Papa squinted up at the sky. "Perhaps we should head for home."

"Are you feeling strong enough for that?" asked Caroline. It was hard enough to tend him here at the fish camp. She didn't want him to collapse when they were halfway home. "Perhaps we should wait until tomorrow."

Papa considered. "Let's start off and see how I do," he said finally. "Your poor mother must be beside herself with worry about you."

He crawled from the shelter, and she helped him get to his feet. He rested an arm across Caroline's shoulders and took one careful step, and then another. "I think I can do it," he said. "Your good care has made a world of difference."

Caroline fetched the crutch she'd made. "Try leaning on this," she said.

The crutch was too long for Papa to use comfortably. Caroline carefully placed it on a rock so that several inches stuck out over the end. *Careful!* she told herself. If she broke off too much, she'd have to search for another stick. That might take a long time.

Caroline held her breath. Then she snapped off the end of the crutch by stamping on it with one foot.

Papa gave it another try. "Perfect!" he said. "Nicely done, Caroline."

Caroline didn't like the way Papa limped, even with the crutch. She didn't like the way he pinched his mouth tight every time he put weight on his right leg.

"If there's any of that fish left, we should eat it now," Papa said. "And then we'll get started."

Caroline hesitated, then nodded. "All right, Papa," she said. "Let's get ready to go."

Twilight and rain fell together that evening as Caroline and Papa inched their way home. Despite the crutch, Papa limped more and more slowly. At one of the farms they passed, a woman gave them each a bowl of stew, but Papa refused her offer to spend the night. "We must get home," he insisted.

As they plodded forward, Papa's chin sagged toward his chest as if he was falling asleep. Caroline tried to keep him awake by telling stories about everything that had happened at home since he'd been captured. She'd gotten to the fishing trip at Hickory Creek by the time they turned from the trail onto the main road to Sackets Harbor. Suddenly Caroline heard a *cra-ack*. Papa stumbled, then went down on one knee. The crutch had broken.

We must rest, Caroline thought. She looked around and pointed to a fallen log near the road. Thick tree branches overhead provided some shelter from the rain. "Let's sit for a moment, Papa."

When they were settled on the log, Papa gave her a weak smile. "So you and Seth and Rhonda had a good fishing trip?" he asked, encouraging her to continue the story.

"Well, no," Caroline confessed. She quickly told him about the British sloop that had tried to capture Irish Jack's bateau. "I knew we needed to block the channel," she said. "But—" Suddenly her voice caught. Part of her was eager to blurt out the truth about destroying the skiff. Part of her didn't want Papa to know.

"What's troubling you, daughter?" Papa asked softly.

"Oh, Papa!" Caroline cried. "To block the channel, we had to sink *Sparrow*! The sloop sailed away and the American supplies were saved, but we lost your skiff. I'm sorry. I had to make a choice

71

very quickly, and . . ." Her voice trailed away.

Papa was quiet for several moments. *He is disappointed in me*, Caroline thought miserably.

Finally Papa said, "I think I know how you feel. When I was a prisoner on that British boat and saw a chance to escape, I had to act very quickly. Diving overboard *might* have been a bad decision. I might have died while I tried to get home. Sometimes, all we can do is take a chance and hope for the best."

Papa did understand! Relief rushed through Caroline. "Well, you are almost home now," she said stoutly. "Let's start walking again."

As they went on their way, Papa leaned more heavily on Caroline. Her knees trembled with the effort of keeping them both moving. It was getting dark, and the rain was falling harder. Soon they would both be soaked. In Papa's weakened state, that might bring back his fever.

Papa was determined, though. *And I'll keep going too*, Caroline promised herself fiercely. "Watch for the ruts, Papa. They're wicked."

It seemed to take forever, but finally Papa and Caroline reached Sackets Harbor. As they turned onto their lane, she heard someone calling her name.

It was Mama! Caroline felt a new burst of energy. "Wait here," she told Papa. "Lean against this tree. I'll get help!"

Papa nodded. Caroline left him and stumbled toward their house. "Here!" she cried.

Mama appeared from the gloom. She carried a lantern, its tiny light flickering like a firefly. She set it down and grabbed Caroline into a crushing hug. "Oh, thank God, thank God," she whispered. "I thought I'd lost you."

Then Mama stepped back. Beneath the edge of her cap, her face was white. "Caroline Abbott, where have you been?" she demanded. "You frightened me out of my wits!"

"I'm so sorry, Mama," Caroline said quickly, "but *please* come with me. We need help!"

"We?" Mama asked, but Caroline was already splashing back through the mud toward Papa. She heard Mama close behind her.

In the dim light, they were almost upon Papa before she heard Mama gasp. "John?" she cried.

Papa opened his arms. "My sweet wife!"

Caroline felt a lump rise in her throat as she watched her parents cling to each other in the rain.

"Thank you, God," she whispered. "Thank you for bringing Papa back to us."

Finally Mama pulled free. She wiped tears and raindrops from her cheeks. "Oh, John, I can scarcely believe it's you!" she said. "But how . . . where . . ."

"I'll tell you the whole story once we're home," Papa promised. "I can say that I wouldn't be here now if Caroline hadn't found me. I was sick and starving and too weak to travel any farther." He put one hand on Caroline's shoulder. "You saved my life, child."

Caroline pressed her cheek against Papa's hand. His words warmed her inside.

Mama looked at Caroline. "How did you ever . . . no, never mind now. I'll hear that story later, too. Now, let's get back to the house." She pulled one of Papa's arms over her shoulders so that she could help support him.

Caroline blinked back tears. It was still hard to believe that Papa was really, truly here!

She knew that the war was far from over. Rhonda's father was away fighting. Caroline's cousin Oliver had joined the navy, and Seth, too. The British might attack Sackets Harbor at any moment.

But those troubles and worries can wait for tomorrow, Caroline thought as she slid her arm around her father's waist. "Lean on me too, Papa," she told him.

Together at last, the Abbott family headed toward home.

LOOKING BACK

GETTING AROUND
IN
1812

A stagecoach carrying travelers through New Jersey in 1811

For people like Caroline's family, traveling even short distances was difficult and often dangerous. Cities and towns had grown up along the Atlantic coast and major eastern lakes and rivers, but only a little farther inland, farms and settlements were just being carved out of the forests. In 1812, Caroline's tiny village of Sackets Harbor, New York, lay on America's northern frontier.

West of the Great Lakes was rugged territory that stretched from Lake Superior all the way to the Pacific Ocean. Native Americans had called this land home for thousands of years, but few non-Indian

These settlers are building a log fence around a new homestead. Caroline would have seen sights like this only a few miles from Sackets Harbor.

The Lewis and Clark expedition set out to find a route to the Pacific in 1803. Native American tribes beyond the Great Lakes had seen few, if any, non-Indians before.

people had ventured there. In fact, the famous Lewis and Clark Expedition—the first United States expedition to reach the Pacific Ocean—was completed only six years before Caroline's story.

Even for people who lived in large cities, getting around was not easy. People who wanted to travel between cities such as Boston, New York, and Philadelphia had only a few choices: they could ride by horse, wagon, or stagecoach along rugged dirt roads, or they could go by boat.

For the Abbotts, who lived far from any city, travel would have been even more difficult. The biggest nearby town, Kingston, was in Upper Canada, a day's sail across Lake Ontario. Before the war broke out in 1812, people on the American side of the lake often traveled there, but large waves and high winds

A stagecoach waits by an inn. Traveling in an open-air coach along rough dirt roads was bumpy and slow.

could push a ship off course. An even greater danger to ships was running aground and breaking up in storms or fog. During winter, ice clogged the harbors, and sailing became impossible for months at a time. When the ice finally

During winter, iced-over harbors kept ships frozen in place.

broke up in spring, people eagerly awaited the first boats of the year, just as Caroline and Mama look for Irish Jack's arrival in the story.

Despite the risks, people traveled by water whenever they could, because going by road was usually even slower and more uncomfortable. On the frontier, there was rarely any place to buy a hot meal or spend the night except a rough, dirty tavern. If a wagon wheel broke or a

horse went lame, there might be no one to help. Rain or melting snow could turn roads to mud and make rivers too deep or fast-running to cross. People preferred to travel overland only in winter, when roads and rivers froze solid.

Travelers often had to cross rivers by riding through them.

During Caroline's time, news traveled the way people did—slowly and unpredictably. A letter could take weeks to get from the East Coast to inland settlements like Sackets Harbor.

Getting mail was a big event. When a post rider galloped into a town, blowing loudly on his horn to announce his arrival, everyone hurried to see what he carried in his pouch. A letter might bring word of a father injured at war or a baby born to an aunt or sister.

A newspaper might carry news of a battle on the high seas or events in faraway Europe. In some places, *post walkers*—often boys like Caroline's friend Seth—were stationed in small towns to carry newspapers and mail even farther, delivering it by hand to outlying farms and villages.

Where Caroline lived, even short walks carried risks. The forest surrounding Sackets Harbor was home to dangerous animals

A post rider blows a horn to let people know that the mail has arrived.

such as cougars, wolves, and bears. The dark, dense woods were also an easy place to get lost. Quick thinking helped Caroline find her way, but other children weren't so lucky. In 1807, one young boy who lived only a few miles from Sackets Harbor went missing on the way to a neighbor's house. Worried townspeople began a search, carrying flaming torches, and horns and guns to signal if the boy were found. Before long, 500 men

Cougars were once common in eastern forests.

and boys had joined the hunt. After three days, searchers stumbled upon the boy in the middle of a swamp, frightened and hungry but very much alive. Men blew their

Forest and swamp in New York

horns and fired their guns into the air, and the forest exploded with joyous shouts. The boy was safe!

Though the forest could be dangerous, it was important to people's survival. Most people lived far from doctors and even

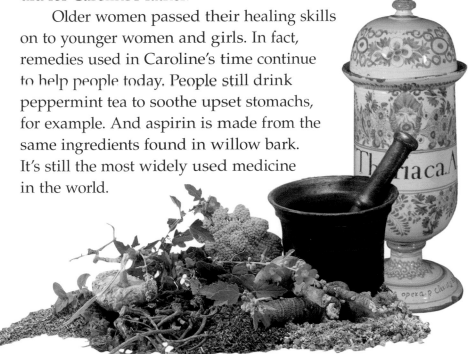

Doctors were scarce, so women became skilled at caring for sick and injured family members.

farther from supplies of store-bought medicines. Women had to make their own medicines when a family member was injured or ill. Much of what they needed came from the woods, where many plants with healing properties could be found. Salve made from the buds of a black walnut tree could soothe an itchy rash. A wildflower called yarrow could slow the bleeding of a bad cut. Tea made from willow bark could cool a raging fever, just as it did for Caroline's father.

Older women passed their healing skills on to younger women and girls. In fact, remedies used in Caroline's time continue to help people today. People still drink peppermint tea to soothe upset stomachs, for example. And aspirin is made from the same ingredients found in willow bark. It's still the most widely used medicine in the world.

Women gathered wild plants and used the roots, leaves, bark, and flowers to make healing remedies.

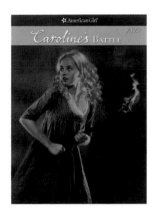

A SNEAK PEEK AT

BATTLE

*When the British attack, Mama and Caroline must guard
Abbott's Shipyard alone. Can Caroline obey the terrible
order that will keep the shipyard out of enemy hands?*

aroline came downstairs at dawn and found Grandmother and Mrs. Hathaway making breakfast. The bacon sizzling over the fire smelled so good that Caroline's stomach growled.

"Please set the dining-room table," Grandmother told Caroline. "Now that your father is home, we've too many people to fit here in the kitchen."

Once everyone had gathered around the table, Caroline introduced the boarders. "Papa, this is Mrs. Hathaway, and Rhonda, and Amelia." She grinned. For months, the Hathaways had heard stories about Papa. Now they could meet him in person!

Little Amelia was very quiet, sucking her thumb and watching him closely. Rhonda seemed unusually shy as well. "A pleasure to meet you, sir," she said. After a quick nod, she looked down at her plate.

Caroline nudged Rhonda under the table with her knee. Usually that would make Rhonda giggle and nudge back even harder. Today, though, Rhonda didn't respond. Caroline was puzzled by her friend's mood.

Suddenly, Caroline realized why Rhonda was being quiet. *Everything's turned upside down,* Caroline thought. *I used to envy Rhonda because her father was nearby.* Now Papa was home, and Rhonda's father was off on a dangerous expedition. Caroline leaned close enough to whisper in her friend's ear. "Your father will be back soon, and—"

Boom! Boom! Caroline looked up sharply and clapped her hands over her ears as cannon fire shuddered through the air. The windowpanes rattled, and it felt as if Caroline's bones rattled, too.

Papa dropped his fork with a clatter. Mama's face paled.

Caroline felt ready to cry. "Those shots came from the big guns at the forts," she said. "Sackets Harbor must be under attack!"

"Under attack?" Papa repeated. His hands curled into fists. His face settled into hard lines.

Caroline jumped to her feet and ran from the dining room and out the front door. She had to find out what was happening! Her family and the Hathaways joined her just as a young man on horseback clattered toward them.

Papa stepped into the street and waved a hand. "Wait!" he barked. "What's happening?"

The young man pulled his horse to a stop. "A British fleet has been sighted about seven miles from here," he told them. "I'm with the militia, on my way to spread the word."

"How large is the fleet?" Papa demanded.

"There are probably a thousand enemy men out there," the militiaman said. "And when they land, they'll have their ships' cannons to protect them."

A thousand men? Caroline felt anger boil up inside. "Hateful British!" she cried, stamping one foot. "I wish they would just leave us *alone!*"

Papa squinted the way he sometimes did when he was sailing a ship and making a judgment about the weather. "There's no wind."

"Aye," the soldier agreed. "Those ships can't move with no wind in their sails. That gives us some time to call in the militia. Now, I must be off!"

He kicked his horse to a gallop, and everyone watched him pound away. Mama murmured, "Thank God the British weren't able to surprise our men."

"But the wind could change again any moment!" Caroline said.

*The young man pulled his horse to a stop. "A British fleet has been sighted.
There are probably a thousand enemy men out there," he told them.*

"It could." Papa nodded. "The wind could pick up again an hour from now or a day from now. In any event, we must use whatever time we have to prepare for their attack."

Grandmother leaned on her cane with both hands. "We've known they would come sooner or later," she said. "They're after that big new warship the navy's building, I'd wager."

"But most of our soldiers and sailors are away!" Rhonda cried. "There's hardly anyone left here to defend us!"

"Those alarm guns were meant to call out the militia," Grandmother reminded Rhonda. "And riders, like that young man we just saw, will be on their way to spread the word to outlying farms, where men might not hear the guns. Our militiamen will be ready to meet the British."

Caroline crossed her arms. She had seen the militia drilling in town, practicing for a battle. The part-time soldiers—local farmers and workmen— were not nearly as well trained as the army and navy men. She understood why Rhonda sounded frightened. Caroline was frightened, too.

"Those British ships can't reach land until the

wind picks up," Mama added. "That may save us. With every passing hour, more militia will arrive in Sackets Harbor."

Another deafening *Boom! Boom!* sounded as the signal guns repeated their message. "Come, girls," Mrs. Hathaway murmured to Rhonda and Amelia.

Caroline glanced at Papa. He looked grim. *What a terrible homecoming!* Caroline thought.

For a long moment, no one spoke. Then Papa turned to his wife. "I must go."

"What?" Mama demanded.

"Go where?" Caroline asked at the same time.

Papa said, "To volunteer with the militia."

"Papa, no!" Caroline cried. How could he leave? She'd just gotten him back!

Mama clutched his arm. "You're not yet well."

"Well enough," Papa said. "I can handle a musket. It's clear that Sackets Harbor needs every man to fight."

Caroline grabbed Papa's free hand. *If I never let go,* she thought, *maybe Papa won't leave.*

READ ALL OF CAROLINE'S STORIES,
available at bookstores and *americangirl.com.*

MEET CAROLINE
When the British attack Caroline's village, she
makes a daring choice that helps to win the day.

CAROLINE'S SECRET MESSAGE
Caroline and Mama take a dangerous journey
to the British fort where Papa is held prisoner.

A SURPRISE FOR CAROLINE
Caroline finds herself on thin ice after
friendship troubles lead to a bad decision.

CAROLINE TAKES A CHANCE
When a warship threatens American supplies,
can Caroline's little fishing boat turn it away?

CAROLINE'S BATTLE
As a battle rages right in her own village,
Caroline faces a terrible choice.

CHANGES FOR CAROLINE
Caroline pitches in on her cousin's new farm—
and comes home to a wonderful surprise.